Secret PRINCESSES

Bunny Surprise

ROSIE BANKS

Wishing Star Palace

The Secret Princess Promise

"I promise that I will be kind and brave,

Using my magic to help and save,

Granting wishes and doing my best,

To make people smile and bring happiness."

CONTENTS

CHAPTER ONE

The Adventure Begins!

"Can we go and feed the ducks, Mummy?" Elsie Thompson tugged at her mum's hand as they walked through the park.

"OK. Let me just grab a coffee from the café first," her mum said.

"Mum!" Elsie whined.

"I'll take Elsie to the pond, Mum," Mia offered helpfully.

"Thanks, sweetheart," said Mrs Thompson, handing Mia a bag of birdseed.

Elsie skipped along beside Mia, her blonde pigtails bouncing as they set off towards the pond. Ducks and fluffy yellow ducklings were paddling around on the surface. "I love ducklings, they're so cute!" she said.

"I like the swans," said Mia, pointing to two elegant white swans who were floating across the water.

"What are those fluffy grey ones?" said Elsie, pointing at the birds paddling along behind the swans.

"They're cygnets – baby swans!" said Mia.

Elsie gave Mia a suspicious look. "They don't look like swans. Are you sure?"

"Positive," said Mia with a laugh. "When they get older they'll get white feathers and their necks will grow long."

"You know *everything* about animals!" Elsie declared.

Mia grinned. She still had lots to learn if she was going to be a vet when she was older, but she loved animals.

She and Elsie threw some birdseed into the water and the ducks squabbled over it. The girls' mum joined them, a coffee in her hand.

"Hey, Mum. What time does a duck wake up?" Mia asked.

"I don't know," said her mum. "When?"

"At the *quack* of dawn!" Mia told her.

Elsie giggled and Mrs Thompson raised her eyebrows. "Hmm. I bet I can guess who told you *that* joke. Was it Charlotte?"

Mia nodded. She and Charlotte had been best friends their whole lives.

When Charlotte had told her that her family was moving to America, Mia had been heartbroken. But just before Charlotte had left, their old babysitter, Alice, had given them matching necklaces. Each necklace was made of gold and had a half-heart pendant on it. The necklaces weren't just pretty – they were magic! They could whisk the girls away to an amazing place called Wishing Star Palace.

But that wasn't the only surprise. When they'd first visited the palace, Alice had explained that Mia and Charlotte had been chosen to train to become Secret Princesses – special people who could grant wishes. If Mia and Charlotte completed all the different stages of training they would become Secret Princesses, just like Alice!

Elsie spotted an ice cream van arriving. "Can we have an ice cream, Mummy?"

"OK," her mum said. "Coming, Mia?"

"Yes, please!" she said. "But can I feed the ducks the rest of the seed first?" Mia had spotted something even more exciting than an ice cream van – her necklace was glowing!

"OK." Her mum and Elise set off. After checking that no one was watching, Mia pulled her pendant out from inside her T-shirt. The half-heart was glowing with light. She was about to have another magical adventure!

"I wish I could see Charlotte!" she whispered, holding the necklace tight.

Light streamed out of the pendant and surrounded her, then swept her away. Mia's heart sang in excitement. Her mum and Elsie wouldn't even know she was gone as no time would pass while she was away — the magic always made sure of that.

Round and round she twirled until she landed on a pebbly beach. The sky was the colour of gorgeous forget-me-nots and little waves lapped against the pebbles of the curving bay. Best of all, her jeans and T-shirt had changed into her beautiful golden princess dress.

"Mia!" Hearing her name, Mia swung round. Charlotte was running across the pebbles towards her. She was wearing a floaty pink dress and a diamond tiara glittered in her curly brown hair.

She gave Mia a huge hug.

"Isn't it great to be back here? I hope we get to make someone's wish come true!" Charlotte said, spinning her round.

Mia hugged her back tightly. "Maybe we'll earn our final rubies!" she said excitedly.

Charlotte held up her half-heart pendant. The three rubies they had already

earned were glittering in the sunlight.

"I hope so, because then we'll pass the second stage of training!"

Mia's face grew serious as she suddenly remembered something else. "I hope we can get Princess Ella's wand back, too."

Princess Ella's wand had been stolen by a green parrot called Venom. He belonged to Princess Poison, a Secret Princess who had turned bad. She loved spoiling people's wishes to get more power. And if Princess Poison used Princess Ella's wand to ruin someone's wish, then poor Ella would be banished from Wishing Star Palace for ever!

Charlotte's eyes flashed with determination and she grabbed Mia's hand. "We *have* to get Ella's wand back."

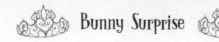

Mia started to nod but then something in the water caught her eye. It was slowly rising out of the water and looked like an enormous bubble, shimmering with all different colours of light.

"What's that?" she said, pointing.

Charlotte stared. "I don't know – but it looks like we're about to find out!"

CHAPTER TWO
Swimming Lesson

The huge bubble drifted to shore and washed up on the pebbles in front of Mia and Charlotte. *POP!* The bubble burst and revealed three princesses – Alice, whose strawberry-blonde hair was streaked with red; Princess Cara, who had curly brown hair and brown eyes; and Princess Ella, whose short black hair gleamed in the light.

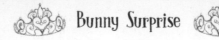

All three princesses were wearing bright-
coloured wetsuits, instead of their usual
elegant dresses.

"Wow! That was so cool!" said Charlotte.

"Hi, girls!" Ella said, hugging them both.
"We thought we'd surprise you."

Alice joined in
with the hug.
"It's lovely to see
you both again."

Mia felt
excitement rush
through her.
"Does someone's
wish need
granting?"

"Not at the moment," said Ella. "We've invited you here today for something more fun – a swimming lesson."

Mia and Charlotte exchanged puzzled looks. What did Ella mean? "Um … OK, but we don't really need lessons," said Mia. "We both know how to swim."

"Aha!" Ella grinned. "But you're not going to be the ones *having* the lesson – you're going to be *giving* it!"

"Today all the seal pups who live on this beach are learning to swim," said Princess Cara. "We're going to help them."

"It's the cutest thing ever," said Alice.

"Oh, wow," breathed Mia. She loved seals, and baby seal pups were even better!

"It sounds awesome!" Charlotte looked down at her princess dress. "But we can't swim in dresses."

"That's easy to solve," said Princess Cara with a giggle. She waved her wand. Mia felt a tingle pass over her skin and suddenly their dresses were replaced with gorgeous coloured wetsuits. Charlotte's was pink and Mia's was gold.

"Look at us!" cried Charlotte.

"Let's go and find the seals," said Ella.

They set off across the beach. Charlotte turned a cartwheel on the pebbles.

"Are the seals over by those pretty rocks?" asked Mia, pointing towards some colourful rocks on the other side of the bay.

Ella chuckled. "Those rocks *are* the seals!"

Mia peered across the beach and began to make out dark eyes and flippers on the seals' pretty pale-pink, lemon, lilac and baby-blue bodies.

"I've never seen seals those colours before!" said Charlotte.

"That's because you only get them here, at Wishing Star Palace," said Ella.

They all hurried closer. As they got nearer, Mia saw that the adult seals had sleek skin and the babies were covered with fluffy fur. They all had enormous round eyes, wrinkled noses and whiskers. The adults were gently nudging the babies towards the water.

"Let's go and help!" said Princess Ella.
The adult seals lifted their heads and barked
a greeting as Ella approached them gently.

Princess Ella stroked a pink seal's head.
"They're very friendly," she told the others
as the seals flapped their flippers in greeting.

Charlotte waded into the water and started encouraging the pup to join her.

Mia spotted a gorgeous lilac-coloured seal further up the beach. The mother seal was barking at her little pup, who was hanging back nervously.

"Hello there," Mia said softly, going over to them. Mia stroked the mother's sleek head. "You're beautiful." The mother seal nuzzled her hand. The baby hid behind her mum's tail and peeped out shyly at Mia, its enormous purple eyes fringed by curling eyelashes.

Mia crouched down and held out her hand. "It's OK, swimming is fun." Mia tickled the pup and it squealed happily.

"I think he likes you, Mia," said Ella. "Why don't you go into the water – maybe he'll follow you."

The baby seal looked at the water uncertainly as Mia waded in. The mother seal wriggled down the stones after her and slid into the waves.

"Want to try swimming?" Mia asked the baby. She stepped a bit further into the water, and the seal pup started wriggling down the beach.

He stopped at the water's edge. "You can do it!" Mia encouraged the baby seal, holding out her arms. The lilac seal pup plunged into the water and swam over to her, nuzzling her hand with his whiskers.

Mia smiled as she watched the pup swim off to play with some of the other babies.

"Isn't this brilliant?" said Charlotte, swimming over and shaking her curls like a dog. "I never thought I'd get to swim with seals!"

"Especially not pink, blue and purple ones," said Mia with a grin.

"Let's play a game!" suggested Alice.

The girls and princesses bobbed down
in the water and began chasing the seals
around, tagging them and then trying
to swim away before the seals could tag
them back.

"You got me!" giggled Mia, as the lilac-
coloured pup tagged her with its soft nose.

At long last, the girls and the princesess waded out of the water and sat on the beach as the seals swam further out to sea. The lilac pup that Mia had helped waved a flipper at her.

Mia waved back and then watched as it swam after the others.

"I'll magic up some towels so we can dry off," said Princess Cara, pulling her wand out of her beach bag. There was a thimble at the end – and it was glowing!

"Someone must have made a wish," said Princess Ella.

Charlotte jumped to her feet. "Can Mia and I try and grant it?"

"Of course," said Alice.

"And we'll do everything we can to get your wand back," Mia promised Ella.

"What's the quickest way for us to get back to the palace?" asked Charlotte.

"I'll use my magic slippers," said Alice. The girls grabbed hands. Alice tapped her heels together and then she and the girls twirled round as they rose into the sky.

"This is amazing!" cried Charlotte as they soared over the palace grounds. She couldn't wait to have ruby slippers of her own, but they needed to earn one more ruby first.

They landed outside a beautiful white palace with four pointed turrets and gorgeous, heart-shaped windows.

They raced through the grand
front door, up a wide
staircase, along a
corridor and into
a tower. At the
very top of the
tower's spiral
staircase was a
round room.
The only
object in the
room was a
full-length mirror on a golden stand.

As they stopped in front of the Magic
Mirror, Mia saw an image of the person
they needed to help. A girl with a pretty

pink headscarf was holding a fluffy grey rabbit and looking wistful. Words appeared on the mirror's surface, under the image.

A wish needs granting, adventures await,
Call Aisha's name, don't hesitate!

"Watch out for Princess Poison," Alice warned. "She'll be doing everything in her power to spoil Aisha's wish."

"We won't let her," said Charlotte.

"Maybe we should try to save one wish for getting Ella's wand back," said Mia.

"That's a great idea," said Charlotte. They had come close to getting the wand back before, but Princess Poison had always

stopped them. They couldn't let that happen again! Charlotte's eyes met Mia's. "Are you ready?"

"Ready," Mia said with a firm nod.

"Aisha!" they both cried. The image in the glass disappeared and was replaced with swirling light.

"Here goes!" cried Charlotte as she and Mia touched the mirror and were swept away into a tunnel of light. They were off to make a wish come true!

CHAPTER THREE

Willow Gets a Fright

Mia and Charlotte whizzed through the
tunnel in a swirling sea of light. They shot
out of the end and landed gently on the
ground. Jumping to their feet, they looked
around. Charlotte was wearing a patterned
jumpsuit and Mia had a pretty blue
dress with bunnies on it, and they were
standing on the pavement of a quiet street.

There were neat front gardens with pretty flowers. Mia could see a man gardening, two boys playing on scooters and a lady walking a little white dog. No one seemed to have noticed the girls' sudden arrival, but that was part of the magic.

"I wonder where Aisha is?" Mia whispered. "We need to find out what her wish is."

"There!" hissed Charlotte, pointing to a front garden a few houses away. The girl from the mirror was sitting on the grass, cuddling a grey rabbit. The front garden was surrounded by a low white fence.

Charlotte hurried over to it. "I like your rabbit," she called, giving the girl a smile. "What's it called?"

Aisha looked up and smiled at them, her brown eyes twinkling. "Hi! This is Willow," she said. "But she's not mine. She belongs to my neighbour, Mr Marvolo."

"Willow's really cute," said Mia.

Aisha smiled again. "I know. Do you want to stroke her?"

Mia and Charlotte nodded eagerly and went through the garden gate. "I'm Aisha," said the girl, putting the rabbit down.

"I'm Charlotte and this is Mia," said Charlotte as Willow hopped over to them. She looked at them, her whiskers twitching and her ears flicking slightly. Mia crouched down and Willow hopped on to her knee.

"She's so friendly," Mia said.

"It's because she met so many children when she was part of Mr Marvolo's act," Aisha explained. "He used to be a magician but he's retired now. Do you have any pets?"

"I have a cat called Flossie," said Mia.

"I haven't," said Charlotte. "My brothers are allergic to fur. But I wish I could. I'd love a rabbit like Willow."

"Me too," said Aisha. "But my mum and dad keep saying I'm not ready. I'm trying to show them that I am by pet-sitting. I walk Mrs Johnson's dog every weekend and I fed my neighbours' cat, Sooty, when they went away. Mr Marvolo asked me to help look after Willow today. I'm going to prove to Mum and Dad that I'm responsible enough to have an animal. I really wish I could have a pet of my own!"

Mia and Charlotte glanced at each other quickly. So now they knew Aisha's wish!

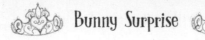

The door of the next house opened and
a man came out. He had a beard and was
dressed in a top hat, a long cape lined with
purple, a white shirt and
a fancy purple bow tie.
"Ah, Aisha, there you
are!" he said, smiling.

"Hi, Mr Marvolo!" Aisha
said, getting to her feet and
smoothing down her long
skirt. She scooped
up Willow and went
over to the fence
that separated her
garden from her
neighbour's.

Mr Marvolo reached over the fence and took Willow from Aisha. "She looks very happy with you," he said. "I think she misses all the cuddles she used to get when we did magic shows for children."

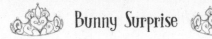

Charlotte frowned. "Excuse me," she said politely. "But if you're a *retired* magician, then why are you still wearing a magician's outfit?"

"Ah, Willow and I are doing a very special birthday party for Aisha's little brother, Ali, later this afternoon," Mr Marvolo said. "The only problem is that I'm a bit rusty because I haven't done some of my magic tricks for a while. Maybe I could practise on you girls?"

"Oh yes!" Charlotte said.

Mr Marvolo tapped his hat thoughtfully. "Now, let me think … I wonder what I could do? What do you think, Willow?"

The girls all looked at the little bunny.

Her whiskers twitched excitedly.

"Maybe I could pull a coin out of her ear," said Mr Marvolo, putting his hand to one of Willow's long ears. "Oh, yes, here we are!" He opened his hand, showing them a coin.

Aisha gasped. "That's brilliant," she cried, reaching out to stroke Willow's ear. "How did you do that?"

Mr Marvolo chuckled. "A magician never reveals his secrets, my dear. Magic is all about making the impossible possible. Maybe I'm not so rusty after all. Now, I'd better go and get the rest of my props. Aisha, would you bring Willow back to my house and make sure she has fresh food and water in her hutch?"

"Of course, Mr Marvolo," said Aisha.

He went back inside.

"How *did* he do that?" wondered Charlotte as she and Mia followed Aisha down the path and into Mr Marvolo's garden. It had a low fence around it and at the side of the house there was a rabbit hutch and a small wooden shed.

"I think he distracted us by getting us to look at Willow," said Mia. "Then he must have got the coin ready quickly and made it look like it had appeared in his hand when he pulled it away from her ear."

Aisha kissed Willow's head. "Would you mind watching Willow while I sort out her food and water?"

"Sure," said Charlotte. She and Mia sat on the grass as the little bunny hopped around the garden, nibbling on the grass. Aisha refilled the water bottle and hay container in Willow's hutch. Then she brought the bag of rabbit pellets out of the shed and began to refill Willow's bowl.

WOOF! WOOF! WOOF!

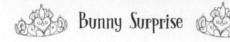

There was the sound of loud barking and snarling outside Mr Marvolo's house. Willow froze. Aisha quickly picked her up.

"It's OK," she soothed, stroking Willow.

"What's going on?" Charlotte shouted above the din.

"Let's go and see," Mia said. She and Charlotte went over to the fence. A small, plump man was standing on the other side with a poodle and an enormous dog with a skull and crossbones on its collar. Both dogs were snarling and pulling on their leads.

"Hex!" exclaimed Mia. Hex was Princess Poison's servant.

Hex smirked. "Yes, it's me! I think Miss Fluffy and Crusher want to play …"

"No! They can't go near Willow, they'll hurt her!" Mia began to protest.

"Whoopsie!" Hex interrupted as he dropped the leads.

"No!" cried Mia as the dogs both jumped into the garden.

Barking loudly, the two dogs raced up the lawn. Luckily, Aisha quickly put Willow in the hutch, fastening the front so the dogs couldn't get at the little bunny. Willow cowered in the straw as the dogs raced around.

"Go away!" Aisha said, standing in front of Willow's hutch protectively.

Crusher seized Willow's food bowl and chomped on it with his massive jaws. Miss Fluffy grabbed the bag of food and shook it from side to side, sending rabbit pellets flying everywhere.

"Stop it!" Mia shouted.

"Bad dogs!"

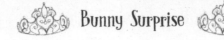

Charlotte looked round desperately. How could they get the dogs out of the garden? Spotting a stick on the grass, she had an idea. She ran and grabbed it. "Fetch!" she cried, throwing the stick so that it sailed over the fence. Crusher and Miss Fluffy raced after it, barking and yapping.

As they jumped the fence, Crusher

spotted a cat on the other side of the road.
He started to chase after it.

"Crusher!" shouted Hex. "Come here!"

With a loud yap, Miss
Fluffy followed Crusher.
Hex set off after them
on his short stubby legs.
"Doggies! Come back!"

"DON'T come back!"
Charlotte shouted after them.

"Poor Willow," said Mia. "I hope
she's OK."

They hurried back up the garden. Aisha
had taken the bunny out of the hutch and
was comforting her. "How dare those dogs
try and hurt Willow!" she said as Mia and

Charlotte rejoined her. Sticking her chin out defiantly, she said, "Now I've got to try and clear up this mess. I won't let them wreck my chances of getting a pet."

"I think we can help you," said Charlotte.

"How?" said Aisha.

"With magic!" said Mia.

Aisha frowned. "But magic isn't real."

Charlotte and Mia exchanged looks.

"Some magic *is* real," said Charlotte. "Just watch!"

CHAPTER FOUR
Real Magic

Charlotte pulled her pendant out of her top.
It was glowing! Mia took her pendant out,
too, and pushed it next to Charlotte's so
that they made a whole heart.

"I wish for a feast for Willow!" said
Charlotte.

With a flash, the mess in the garden
vanished. A new bag of rabbit pellets

appeared, along with a purple bowl which had Willow's name written on to it in sparkly writing. There was a pile of fresh vegetables, just right for a rabbit – carrots, lettuce leaves and radishes.

"What … what just happened?" Aisha asked faintly.

Willow wriggled in Aisha's arms. Aisha put her down and watched her hop to the pile of fresh vegetables.

"It's magic," said Charlotte.

"*Real* magic."

"We're
training to
be Secret
Princesses,"
Mia
explained.
"We help make
people's wishes
come true!"

Aisha gaped at her.

"But only the person we're trying to help
can know our secret," said Charlotte.

"Um, but won't Mr Marvolo think it's
weird when he sees the new bowl and all
these vegetables?" said Aisha.

"He won't notice," said Charlotte. "That's how the magic works." She grinned. "It's really awesome."

Aisha looked as if she could hardly believe it. "So you're here to help my wish come true," she worked out. "My wish to have a pet of my own."

Mia nodded. "But our magic isn't strong enough to just grant your wish and give you a pet — we have three small wishes that we can use to help you. And there's something else you should know. There's a horrible lady called Princess Poison who will try and stop us. Those dogs belonged to her. She'll do anything she can to spoil your wish."

Aisha screwed her face up at the thought.

"Well, she's not going to stop me from taking good care of Willow," she said. "I'm just going to go inside and get her some more water."

"She's really brave," said Mia, as Aisha went into the house.

"We won't let Princess Poison spoil her wish!" Charlotte declared.

"Oh, really?" Princess Poison's voice snapped through the air. The girls swung round and saw a tall, thin woman looking over the fence. Her green eyes glittered icily. Pulling a wand with a paw print at the end out of her pocket, Princess Poison twirled it tauntingly. "You seem to forget that I've got your precious friend's wand."

Charlotte marched towards her crossly. "Give that wand back. It's Princess Ella's, not yours."

Princess Poison whipped the wand out of Charlotte's reach. "Poor Princess Ella," she mocked. "When I spoil your new friend's wish with her wand, Ella will be banished from the palace. Though at least she'll have *you* to keep her company.

You'll get kicked out too when you don't grant this wish and fail the second stage of your training!" She cackled and pointed the wand at Willow's hutch.

**"Wand of magic, at the double,
Break this hutch, cause lots of trouble!"**

With a loud crack, Willow's hutch fell into pieces! Princess Poison shrieked with laughter. "When that magician sees this, he's not going to be happy at all!

And Aisha's parents will never let her get a pet when they hear that she destroyed the rabbit's hutch." She put her hand to her ear. "Oh, is that the magician coming now? Bye, bye, my dears. I must dash!"

Still cackling, she disappeared in a flash of green light.

Mia heard footsteps behind her. *Oh no!* she thought. She turned round, expecting to see Mr Marvolo.

Luckily, it was Aisha, holding Willow's water bottle. She stared at the ruined hutch in dismay.

"Let me guess," she said, her brown eyes flashing. "Did that mean princess do this?"

Mia nodded. "Yes, it was Princess Poison."

"Don't worry, we'll use another wish. We've still got two left," said Charlotte. She and Mia pressed their pendants together.

"I wish for an amazing new hutch for Willow!" said Mia quickly.

Light shot out of the pendants and hit the broken hutch. The pieces vanished and a luxury rabbit hutch appeared. The new hutch had three storeys with ramps leading from floor to floor. There were chew toys on the two upper floors and a snug sleeping area on the ground floor. Instead of a water bottle there was a miniature water fountain. The outside was decorated with colourful bunting and there was a large sign on the roof with a picture of a carrot on it.

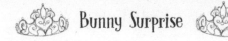

A rabbit flap led to an outside area, planted with a maze of tunnels for her to play in.

"What a gorgeous hutch!" gasped Aisha. "Willow will love it!"

They'd made the wish just in time. The door opened and Mr Marvolo came out.

He was pushing a trolley that had four wheels and curtained sides. The magician didn't seem surprised to see the new hutch, he just smiled kindly. "It looks like Willow is tucking into a real feast," he said. "You're looking after her wonderfully well, Aisha. Thank you so much, my dear."

Aisha beamed.

Mia took Charlotte aside and whispered, "Willow's new hutch is great, but now we only have one wish left. We really need to try and save it for getting Ella's wand back."

Charlotte nodded. "We'll just have to find other ways to grant Aisha's wish."

"Now, girls, I'm going to get everything set up for the party," said Mr Marvolo.

"Aisha, would you please put Willow in her carrier and bring her round for me?"

"Of course," said Aisha. Once Willow was happily settled in her carrier with a carrot to munch on, the girls went next door to Aisha's house.

"I'll ask if you can stay for my brother's party," said Aisha. "I'm sure Mum and Dad won't mind."

"We can watch out for Princess Poison as well," Charlotte murmured to Mia.

"If we do see her, we must try and get Ella's wand back," said Mia.

Charlotte nodded. "But how? It's impossible. We never get close enough to her to try and grab it."

Mia frowned slightly. Charlotte's words had reminded her of something. "What had Mr Marvolo said? 'Magic makes the impossible possible.'"

Charlotte looked thoughtful. "Hmm. Maybe you're right."

Mia squeezed her hand. "We'll think up a plan. We're going to make sure Aisha's wish is granted *and* get that wand back, no matter what!"

Aisha's mum was bustling around making last-minute preparations for the party. She wore a colourful headscarf like Aisha's, and a loose, long-sleeved top and trousers.

"Mummy," Aisha said. "This is Charlotte and Mia. Is it OK if they stay for the party?"

"Yes, that's fine," said her mum.

"Thank you. We're happy to help out," said Charlotte.

"Hopefully there won't be too much to do," said Aisha's dad, who had the same warm brown eyes as his daughter. "The food is all ready and I think the marvellous Mr Marvolo will keep the boys entertained. Ali is very excited about having a real life magician at his party."

"Did I hear my name?" Mr Marvolo poked his head through the patio doors.

"I was just saying I'm sure you have plenty of tricks up your sleeve to amuse the boys," said Aisha's dad with a chuckle.

Mr Marvolo gave a grin. "Indeed I do.

Now, Aisha, would you bring Willow
through to the back garden?" He turned to
her parents. "I must tell you that Aisha
is doing a simply wonderful job of looking
after Willow."

Aisha's eyes glowed with pride as she
followed Mr Marvolo into the garden with
Mia and Charlotte.

Mr Marvolo had parked his trolley in the
garden under a striped gazebo. The trolley's
sides were draped with sparkly purple velvet
so that the audience couldn't see the props
hidden on its shelves. Next to the trolley
was a huge black trunk with gold locks.
Aisha put Willow's carrier gently down
behind the trunk.

"Perhaps you would be kind enough to let me practise another trick on you," Mr Marvolo said, pulling a deck of cards out of one of his pockets. They nodded eagerly.

He spread the cards out in his hand.
"Right! Please pick a card and show it to
me, Mia," he said.

Mia selected a card and showed Mr
Marvolo what it was.

"Aha, the queen of hearts," he said. "Now,
if you would be so good as to place it face
down on the trunk?"

Mr Marvolo pulled his magician's wand
out and waved it in elaborate circles in
the air over the cards. "Abracadabra!" He
tapped the card then turned it the right way
up. It was now the seven of diamonds.

"The card changed!" said Mia in surprise.

"How did you do it?" asked Charlotte.

The magician tapped his nose twice.

"I'm sworn to secrecy," he said.

"I think you distracted us by waving your wand," said Aisha.

Mr Marvolo winked. "Or maybe it was just magic."

"Aisha! Ali! The guests are starting to arrive!" called Aisha's mother.

Charlotte and Mia helped by handing round drinks while Aisha piled up the birthday presents the guests had bought and her mum and dad chatted to the parents.

"Aisha, can you check if Mr Marvolo is ready yet?" Aisha's dad asked.

The girls all hurried into the garden. "Mr Marvolo? Are you ready?" Aisha called.

"Very nearly," he said. "Could you get

Willow out for me, please. I need her for my famous hat trick."

Aisha bent down to open the bunny carrier. She gasped.

"What is it?" asked Mia.

Aisha stared up at her, her brown eyes wide. "Willow's gone! The carrier door was open!"

"What?" cried Mr Marvolo. "Didn't you close it properly, Aisha?"

"I did!" Aisha insisted. "I know I did!"

"I'll go and check whether she went back to her hutch," said Mr Marvolo, heading back to his own garden.

There was a triumphant squawk from a nearby tree. Charlotte looked up. "It's Venom!" she cried, pointing at Princess Poison's pet.

Mia followed her gaze and saw the green parrot sitting in the tree. Her heart sank. "Now we know how Willow got out," she said. The parrot's curved beak could have easily opened the carrier.

"We need to find her," said Aisha. "Willow might be in danger!"

CHAPTER FIVE
Princess Poison's Trick

Mia, Charlotte and Aisha began to search around the garden. "Maybe Willow is hiding in a hedge or a flowerbed?" said Mia.

They searched the bushes and shrubs, pushing aside the leaves.

"Oh, where is she?" said Aisha. "What if she's hopped away and we never find her?"

"We'll find her," Mia said comfortingly.

"There are some paw prints over here,"
said Charlotte, pointing to some soft soil
near the gazebo. She followed the paw
prints but they disappeared into the grass.

Mia thought hard – where might a rabbit
hide? Rabbits liked dark places where they
could burrow. She pulled open the curtains
of the trolley.

As Mia pushed aside a pile of scarves
on the bottom shelf she caught sight of a
splodge of grey fur. "Look!" She pulled out
the scarves and revealed the little rabbit.

"Willow!" cried Aisha. She raced over
and picked up the bunny. "Oh, I'm so glad
we've found you!"

"Thank goodness," said Mr Marvolo,
hurrying back from his garden. Just then,
the patio doors opened and ten boys came
running out. They were led by Ali, who had
dark brown hair. Pinned to his T-shirt was a
badge with 'five today' on it.

"Come and sit down!" Mr Marvolo called
to the party guests. He reached for Willow.
"I'll take her now, Aisha."

Aisha handed Willow over. As the magician got ready to start the show, the three girls joined the crowd of excited boys. "Welcome, all of you!" said Mr Marvolo, taking his hat off and bowing to his audience. "Prepare to be amazed!"

He pulled out a handkerchief from his pocket. "Now, let me see, have I got one handkerchief here? No. I have two, three, four …" He kept pulling them out of his pocket in a long stream. The boys laughed.

Mr Marvolo performed card tricks, made metal rings link together, made watches vanish then reappear and pulled coins out of people's ears. Ali and all his party guests got a turn at being the magician's assistant.

Watching very carefully, Mia could see how he distracted the audience by talking to them and waving his wand while he quickly swapped things round and pulled objects out of his sleeves.

"Maybe we could use our last wish to distract Princess Poison so we can get Ella's wand back," Mia whispered to Charlotte.

Charlotte nodded. "Good idea."

Mia glanced around. For the first time ever she *wanted* Princess Poison to appear!

Finally, Mr Marvolo reached his grand finale. "And now, for my last trick, I shall pull a rabbit out of my hat!" he declared, twirling his wand in his hand. He swept his hat off his head and showed the inside

to the audience. "I think you will all agree
that this hat is empty. Well, with magic,
that will all change and a rabbit will
appear! However, I need a very special
assistant for this final trick. Aisha, would
you kindly join me up here?"

Aisha went to stand beside him.

Mia exchanged smiles with Charlotte.
But as she did so, she caught her breath.
Princess Poison and Hex had appeared on
the other side of the garden fence and were
watching Mr Marvolo with horrid smirks on
their faces.

"Look!" Mia hissed, nudging Charlotte.

Charlotte's eyes widened. "This could be
our chance to get Ella's wand!"

"But we can't just do it in the middle of the show," Mia whispered. "We'll have to wait until Mr Marvolo's finished."

Mr Marvolo held his wand out to Aisha. "Now my dear, I would like you tap my hat three times and say 'Abracadabra!'"

Aisha took his wand and tapped the hat three times. As she did so, Mia saw Princess Poison pull out Ella's wand. There was a flash of green light. Mia clutched Charlotte's arm. "Charlotte, Princess Poison has just cast a spell!"

"What's she done?" said Charlotte.

"Abracadabra!" Aisha cried.

Mr Marvolo reached into the top hat. His fingers scrabbled around.

"Where's the rabbit?" Ali called.

"Um, she must be here somewhere," said Mr Marvolo, looking anxious. "Maybe you could say the magic words again, Aisha."

"This is boring!" complained another little boy.

"Abracadabra!" said Aisha desperately. She tapped the top hat again.

"Mia!" hissed Charlotte. "Princess Poison must have done something to make Willow really disappear."

"We need to use our third wish!" said Mia. She held her pendant up. It was glowing very faintly.

"But we were saving it to get Princess Ella's wand back," said Charlotte.

"We don't have a choice," said Mia. "We can't let Princess Poison ruin Ali's party. And we've got to get Willow back!"

Charlotte pushed her pendant against Mia's. "I wish Willow would appear in a really amazing way!" she whispered.

There was a bright flash of light. The audience blinked and then cried out in amazement. Willow had suddenly appeared in Aisha's arms, wearing a miniature top hat that matched Mr Marvolo's!

The boys all jumped up and cheered. Mr Marvolo blinked several times. Even Charlotte and Mia couldn't help clapping. The magic had worked!

Aisha gasped and kissed the bunny's head.

"Oh, Willow. I'm so glad you're OK!" she muttered into the rabbit's soft fur.

Mr Marvolo's face broke into a warm smile.

"And that, my dears, is the end of the show," he said bowing. "Aisha, would you like to take a bow, too?"

Aisha bowed and waved Willow's paw.

The boys clapped and whooped and
then Aisha's parents came up to the front.
"Thank you so much, Mr Marvolo," said
Aisha's mum. "Now, boys, it's time for tea!"

"Food! Yum!" Ali jumped to his feet and
raced inside with his friends following him.

"That was a really excellent magic
show, Mr Marvolo," said Aisha's dad. He
chuckled. "You almost fooled me with
that last trick. I thought something had
gone wrong. How did you get the rabbit to
appear in Aisha's arms out of thin air?"

"Ah, we magicians must keep our
secrets," he said, looking a little flustered.
"The important thing is that the children
enjoyed it." He turned to Aisha and stroked

Willow's ears. "You've enjoyed it too, haven't you, Willow? Aisha has taken very good care of you."

Aisha hugged the bunny. "I love looking after her. I'd love a pet of my own."

Mr Marvolo looked at her for a moment. "What would you say, my dear, to having *Willow* as your pet?"

Aisha looked confused. "You mean a bunny like Willow?"

"No, my dear," said Mr Marvolo kindly. "I mean, would you like to have Willow? I can't play with her as much as I used to, and she misses being around children. Today I realised how happy she would be with you." He glanced at Aisha's parents.

"Would you let Aisha keep Willow? You could have her hutch and things as well."

Aisha's dad scratched his beard. "It's a very kind offer, Mr Marvolo, but we hadn't planned on Aisha getting a pet quite so soon. We're not sure she's old enough."

"Nonsense!" said Mr Marvolo. "Age has nothing to do with it. Aisha is one of the most responsible girls I have ever met. She always looks after Willow wonderfully."

Aisha turned to her parents. "Oh, please let me have Willow. Please! I *am* ready. I've been a really good petsitter and I promise I'd look after her ..."

Her mum and dad looked at each other and then to Mia's delight they smiled.

"All right, Aisha," said her mother. "You've proved that you're ready to be a pet owner. But Mr Marvolo, are you sure this is what you want?"

"Absolutely," he declared.

"Then yes, Aisha, you can have Willow," said her dad. Smiling at Mr Marvolo, he added, "And you can come and visit Willow any time you like."

Aisha squealed in delight, making Willow's ears twitch in surprise.

Charlotte grabbed Mia's arm. "Her wish has come true!"

At that, six beautiful white doves suddenly burst out of Mr Marvolo's top hat and flew into the air.

"Even more magic!" beamed Aisha's dad. "Mr Marvolo, you really are full of surprises!"

Mr Marvolo turned his hat this way and that. Mia could tell he was just as surprised as Aisha's dad!

"Come on, let's go inside and get something to eat," said Aisha's mum. The adults all headed indoors.

"We just need to get Ella's wand back now," said Mia.

Charlotte looked round. "But where's Princess Poison? She's disappeared."

Mia's heart sank as she realised that Charlotte was right. Princess Poison and Hex were no longer standing by the garden fence. Now what were they going to do? They had to get Ella's wand back – and they'd used all their magic!

Aisha came over to them. "My wish came true and it's all because of you two!" she said, her eyes shining. "Thank you both so much!"

"I'm really glad you get to keep Willow," said Mia, stroking the adorable bunny.

Charlotte nodded. "You're really lucky."

"I'll take good care of her," said Aisha.

She looked at the magician's wand she
was still holding. "I didn't believe in magic
before, but now I know it *is* real."

"Oh, it's real all right," hissed a voice.
They looked round and saw that Princess
Poison had appeared in the garden with
Hex. She pointed her finger at Willow.
"And you and your little bunny friend are
about to find out just how real it can get!"

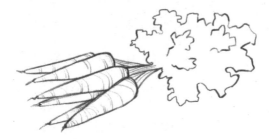

CHAPTER SIX
Ruby Slippers

Aisha gasped in alarm. "Please don't hurt Willow!"

Mia pulled Charlotte to one side. "What are we going to do?" she whispered. "We don't have any wishes left."

"We need to stick to the plan," Charlotte whispered back. "We'll distract her – then we can try and swap the wand."

But where *was* Ella's wand?

"We're not scared of you, Princess Poison," taunted Charlotte. "We've granted Aisha's wish, and there's nothing you can do about it. So, ha ha!"

"Oh, really," Princess Poison sneered. "Shall I turn her fluffy little bunny into a toad? Or a slug maybe?"

"What are you doing?" Mia whispered to Charlotte. "She might use Ella's wand to hurt Willow – and we won't be able to stop her."

"We can't get the wand until we know where it is,"

Charlotte whispered back.

Provoking Princess Poison was a risky plan – but Mia trusted her best friend.

"Please turn that silly bunny into a slug!" pleaded Hex, his beady eyes gleaming.

Aisha bravely brandished Mr Marvolo's wand at Princess Poison. "You stay away from Willow!"

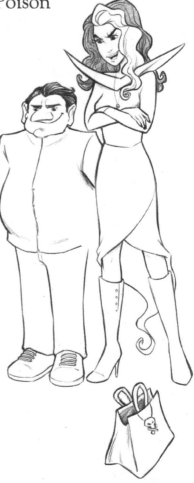

"Don't worry, Aisha," Charlotte said loudly. "She wouldn't dare. Nobody's going to be turning Willow into anything!"

Princess Poison looked down her nose at her. "Oh really? And how exactly do you plan on stopping me? I know you haven't got any magic left in your pendants. Whereas I …" Her green eyes flashed. "I have your princess friend's wand." She opened her handbag. "And now is the perfect time to use it!"

Mia's heart raced. Here was their chance!

"We might not have any magic," said Charlotte, "but—"

Just then, Mia shrieked. "Princess Poison, look!" She pointed behind the princess.

"What *is* Venom doing?"

"My parrot? Where?" snapped Princess Poison, looking behind her. "I told him to go home." Shielding her eyes from the sun, she looked up into the trees. "I can't see anything."

"There! There!" cried Charlotte loudly, waving her arms wildly. Hex turned too. Charlotte rushed over to the tree and started jumping up and down.

Mia knew she had to act – and fast! Her heart beating fast, she grabbed Mr Marvolo's wand from Aisha and darted forwards. While Princess Poison and Hex were distracted, she plucked Ella's wand out from Princess Poison's handbag.

Then she slipped Mr Marvolo's wand inside
and leapt back, her heart beating fast.

"You silly girl, you're imagining things!"
Princess Poison snapped at Charlotte.
"Well, I'm not wasting any more time on
your games. I am going to cast my spell."

Without looking down, she pulled Mr
Marvolo's wand out of her bag. "I shall turn
that bunny into a snake and then I shall
look forward to spoiling hundreds more
animal wishes with Princess Ella's wand!"

Charlotte came back into the garden.
She raised her eyebrows at Mia, who
nodded, a grin spreading over her face.

"Oh, I don't think you will!" Charlotte
said, with a grin.

"But go ahead and try if you want,"
added Mia.

Princess Poison frowned, clearly taken
aback. "What do you mean?"

"Mistress! The wand!" exclaimed Hex, his
eyes bulging.

Princess
Poison
looked at the
fake wand in
her hand.
No!" she
shrieked. "How
did this happen?"

Charlotte's
eyes twinkled.
"Magic, of course!"

Mia held up Princess Ella's wand
triumphantly. "Princess Ella's wand will
only be used for good, and no one can
banish her from the palace!"

Princess Poison screamed in fury.

"But mistress, you said we'd keep the wand," Hex began. "You said—"

"Shut up, you fool!" shrieked Princess Poison. "This was all your fault. You should have been watching them! You may have won this time," she snarled at the girls. "But I shall be back! You haven't seen the last of Princess Poison, I can promise you that!" She clapped her hands and then she and Hex vanished in a flash of green light.

There was a moment of sudden silence.

"We did it," Mia said, her breath leaving her in a rush.

"We really did," said Charlotte, taking Mia's hand. "We make a great team."

Aisha beamed at them. "You really do!"

"Girls!" Aisha's mum called out from the patio. "Are you coming to get some food? If you're not quick, Ali and the boys will eat it all!"

"Coming!" Aisha called.

"Actually, we should be going," said Charlotte. "Can you tell your mum we had to leave?"

Aisha looked sad. "OK, but I wish you could stay. It's been so much fun hanging out with you."

Charlotte hugged her. "We've had lots of fun, too."

Mia stroked Willow's forehead. "Look after Willow, OK?"

"I will," Aisha promised happily.

Giving the girls one last smile, she turned and went inside.

A moment later there was a flash of light and Princess Ella appeared.

"Ella!" cried Charlotte. "Guess what? We've got your wand!"

Ella hugged them. "Thank you so much. I was watching everything in the Magic Mirror. You've been so brave and clever." Charlotte handed the wand to her and Ella sighed in delight. "My wand! The first thing I'm going to do with it is *this!*" She touched the paw print at the end of her wand to Charlotte and Mia's necklaces. There was a bright red flash and a ruby appeared in each of their pendants.

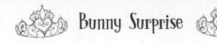

"Our fourth ruby!" said Mia.

"Does that mean we've completed
the second stage of our training?" asked
Charlotte, breathlessly.

Princess Ella smiled. "Let's find out!" She waved her wand around their heads. Light trailed out of it, wrapping them in a magic circle, and then the girls felt themselves being whisked away.

They landed in the grand entrance hall of Wishing Star Palace, back in their princess dresses. All the other princesses cheered and clapped as they appeared.

"You did it!" cried Alice, running over to them and hugging them both tightly. "I'm so proud of you!"

"We're all proud of you," said Princess Anna, an older princess with a silvery grey bun. She smiled warmly at the girls and pointed her wand at their feet.

"Kindness and friendship will never lose,
Rubies now change to glittering shoes!"

Sparkles flew out of her wand. The four
rubies in their pendants vanished and their
shoes changed into beautiful ruby slippers.

"They're gorgeous!" cried Charlotte.

Mia tilted her foot to the side, watching
the light dance across the rubies. The
sparkling slippers felt as light as air. Mia
tingled with excitement.

"You'll wear them every time you visit
Wishing Star Palace," said Alice.

"That is, if both of you wish to continue
your training," said Princess Anna.

"Yes, of course we do!" Mia burst out.

She and Charlotte danced in delight.

"Excellent! For your next stage of training, you must grant four more wishes and earn four sapphires," said Princess Anna.

"Then you'll get your magic princess rings," added Alice. "They'll glow to warn you of danger."

Mia and Charlotte's eyes met. "We'll do it," Charlotte said.

Mia nodded. Nothing was going to stop them from becoming Secret Princesses!

Princess Ella said, "I propose a toast!" She waved her wand and suddenly everyone was holding a crystal glass.

"To Mia and Charlotte!" cried Princess Ella, raising her glass.

"Mia and Charlotte!" cried the others. Mia smiled round at everyone and sipped the delicious drink, which tasted just like yummy fizzy strawberries.

"Now, I'm afraid it's time for you to go home," said Alice when they had finished their drinks. "But it means you can try out your new shoes! Just click the heels together and think about where you want to go." She hugged them. "See you both very soon!"

"Bye, everyone!" called Charlotte and Mia, waving.

Charlotte looked at Mia. "Ready?"

Mia nodded and they clicked their heels at the same time.

Home, thought Mia, picturing the park where she had left her mum and Elsie.

She gasped as she felt herself being lifted into the air and the next moment she was spinning away.

She caught a few brief glances of the Wishing Star Palace grounds – the carousel, the summerhouse, the bay where the colourful seals were splashing in the blue water and then everything blurred and she didn't see anything apart from sparkles until her feet landed on soft grass. She could hear birdsong and laughter. She was back in the park by the pond and her ruby slippers had changed back into her trainers.

Mia blinked and rubbed her face. She spotted her mum and Elsie heading towards the ice cream van and ran to join them.

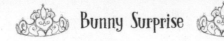

"What ice lolly do you want, girls?" her mum asked.

Elsie bounced up and down eagerly. "I want a rocket lolly. I wish I had a real rocket and could zoom up into the sky!"

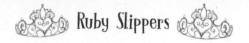

"That would be fun," her mum said.

Mia smiled to herself. She and Charlotte didn't need a rocket to fly into the sky, they just needed their ruby slippers!

Happiness fizzed through her as she thought about all the amazing places they would visit together using their magic princess slippers. There was nothing better than helping the Secret Princesses and having adventures with her best friend – absolutely nothing at all!

The End

Join Charlotte and Mia in their next Secret Princesses adventure

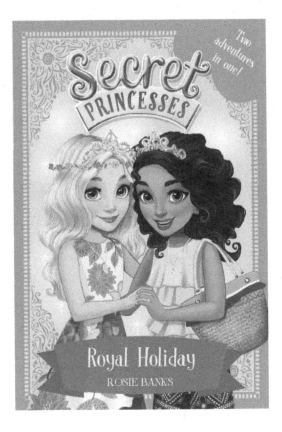

Read on for a sneak peek!

Royal Holiday

"Is there any more chilli, Dad?" Charlotte Williams asked, scooping up the last of her dinner. "It's really yummy!"

"There is something about a campfire that makes everything taste better," her father said with a smile, spooning another helping of the spicy stew onto Charlotte's plastic plate.

"Me too!" said her little brother, Liam.

"Me three!" piped up his twin, Harvey.

"I guess everyone worked up an appetite today," Charlotte's mother said, chuckling.

Charlotte and her family were on a summer holiday in Arizona. They had driven all the way there from their home in California. Today they had hiked down to the bottom of the Grand Canyon, where they were camping overnight. The hike had been amazing, but Charlotte's legs were really tired now!

Charlotte gazed around her. The canyon's steep rock walls glowed orange in the sunset, and the sky was a dusky purple, streaked with pink clouds. She'd thought the desert would be dry and dusty, but it was bursting with colour and life.

"Look!" cried Harvey. "A lizard!"

A little lizard scuttled past over the rocks.

"Can I borrow your phone, Mum?" Charlotte asked. "I want to take a picture to show Mia."

Charlotte quickly snapped a photo of the lizard as it basked on a rock. Then she took a selfie of herself with the canyon in the background, her brown curls shining in the setting sun's rays.

"You can email those to Mia when we get home," Charlotte's mum said. "I'm sure you'll have lots to tell her."

Mia Thompson was Charlotte's best friend, who lived in England. She loved all animals – even scaly reptiles – and knew lots about them. Not long ago, Charlotte's family had moved to California. She'd been really sad to leave her best friend, but they still spoke all the time.

When everyone had finished their chilli, Liam yawned and Harvey rubbed his eyes.

Dad stood up and put out the campfire. "I think we all need an early night," he said.

They carried their plates and cutlery into the cosy log cabin where they were spending the night. After washing the dishes, Charlotte and her brothers got ready for bed.

Soon, Liam and Harvey were snoring softly, but Charlotte couldn't sleep. There were so many things she wanted to tell Mia about – the rafting trip they'd taken, the eagle she'd seen soaring in the sky, and how Harvey had accidentally sat on a cactus!

But maybe she wouldn't have to email her, because Charlotte and her best friend shared a wonderful secret ... they were training to become Secret Princesses, who used magic to make people's wishes come true!

Charlotte felt under her pyjama top and pulled out a gold necklace with a pendant shaped like half a heart. Mia had a matching necklace, with the other half of the heart. Charlotte peeked under the bedcovers and her heart pounded with excitement. Her pendant was glowing!

Holding the pendant, Charlotte whispered, "I wish I could see Mia."

The light from the pendant grew brighter and swirled around Charlotte. She felt herself being swept away from the cabin, but she wasn't worried about her family missing her. Thanks to the magic, no time would pass here while she was gone.

A moment later, Charlotte landed on a lush, green lawn. Her pyjamas had been transformed into a floaty pink princess dress and a diamond tiara rested on her curls. Wishing Star Palace rose up from the clouds, pink roses climbing up its white walls and purple flags fluttering from its four towers.

Even though she had come here before, Charlotte couldn't help gasping. The palace looked so beautiful, especially on a lovely, sunny day. But the best sight of all was a girl with long, blonde hair, who was there studying a note pinned to the palace's door.

"Mia!" cried Charlotte, running over to hug her best friend.

Read Royal Holiday
to find out what
happens next!

Princess Ella's Rabbit Care Tips

Gentle, friendly and fluffy – rabbits are popular pets. But owning a rabbit is more work than you might think. Here, Princess Ella tells you what rabbits need to stay healthy and happy.

- Always make sure your rabbit has plenty of clean water to drink.

- Feed your rabbit hay, with a few fresh vegetables. Carrots, celery, spinach and broccoli are all good for rabbits to nibble – but make sure to wash them first. Avoid giving your rabbit cereal-based food as it is high in sugar.

- Rabbits can live indoors or outdoors, but whatever type of house you choose make sure it is safe from predators and that your pet has plenty of room to stretch out and hop around.

- Check your rabbit's bedding every day. If it's dirty, change it. You can even litter train your rabbit!

Equipment List:

- Heavy food and water bowls

- Carrier

- Brush

- House and bedding

- Litter box and rabbit litter

- Toys

Dos and Don'ts

DO consider getting two rabbits. They get lonely and like to have company!

DON'T put your rabbit in the same cage as a guinea pig. The rabbit could hurt the guinea pig.

DO give outdoor rabbits extra bedding and cold weather protection during the winter months.

DON'T get a rabbit unless you are willing to make a long-term commitment. Rabbits can live for ten years!

♥ FREE NECKLACE ♥

In every book of Secret Princesses series two:
The Ruby Collection, there is a special Wish Token.
Collect all four tokens to get an exclusive Best Friends
necklace for you and your best friend!

Simply fill in the form below, send it in with your four tokens
and we'll send you your special necklaces.*

Send to: Secret Princesses Wish Token Offer, Hachette Children's Books
Marketing Department, Carmelite House, 50 Victoria Embankment,
London, EC4Y 0DZ

Closing Date: 31st June 2017

secretprincessesbooks.co.uk

✂- -

Please complete using capital letters (UK and Republic of Ireland residents only)

FIRST NAME:

SURNAME:

DATE OF BIRTH: DD MM YYYY

ADDRESS LINE 1:

ADDRESS LINE 2:

ADDRESS LINE 3:

POSTCODE:

PARENT OR GUARDIAN'S EMAIL ADDRESS:

I'd like to receive regular Secret Princesses email newsletters and information about other great Hachette Children's Group offers (I can unsubscribe at any time).

Terms and Conditions apply. For full terms and conditions please go to secretprincessesbooks.co.uk/terms

1 Secret Princesses Wish Token

* 2000 necklaces available while stock
Terms and conditions apply.

♥ WIN A PRINCESS GOODY BAG ♥

Secret PRINCESSES
What would you wish for?

Design your own dress and win a Secret Princesses goody bag for you and your best friend!

Charlotte and Mia get to wear beautiful dresses at Wishing Star Palace, but now they want you to design one for them.

To enter all you have to do is follow these steps:

Go to **www.secretprincessesbooks.co.uk**

♥ Click the competition module
♥ Download and print the activity sheet
♥ Design a beautiful dress for Charlotte or Mia
♥ Send your entry to:

Secret Princesses: Ruby Collection Competition
Hachette Children's Group
Carmelite House
50 Victoria Embankment
London
EC4Y 0DZ

Closing date: 31st March 2017
For full terms and conditions,
visit www.hachettechildrens.co.uk/terms

Good luck!

Secret PRINCESSES

What would you wish for?

Are you a Secret Princess?
Join the Secret Princesses Club at:

secretprincessesbooks.co.uk

Explore the magic of the
Secret Princesses and discover:

♥ Special competitions! ♥
♥ Exclusive content! ♥
♥ All the latest princess news! ♥

Ruby820

Enter the special code above on the website to receive

50 Princess Points